HORRID
HENRY
ROCKS

Meet HORRID HENRY the laugh-out-loud worldwide sensation!

....

* Over 15 million copies sold in 27 countries and counting

* # 1 chapter book series in the UK

* Francesca Simon is the only American author to ever win the Galaxy British Book Awards Children's Book of the year (past winners include J. K. Rowling, Philip Pullman, and Eoin Colfer).

"A loveable bad boy."

—People

"Horrid Henry is a fabulous antihero...**a modern comic classic**." —*Guardian*

"**Wonderfully appealing to girls and boys alike**, a precious rarity at this age." —Judith Woods, *Times*

"The best children's comic writer."
—Amanda Craig, *Times*

"**I love the Horrid Henry books by Francesca Simon**. They have lots of funny bits in. And Henry always gets into trouble!" —Mia, age 6

"My two boys love this book, and **I have actually had tears running down my face and had to stop reading because of laughing so hard**." —T. Franklin, parent

"**Fine fare for beginning readers**, this clever book should find a ready audience." —*Booklist*

"**The angle here is spot-on, and reluctant readers will especially find lots to love about this early chapter book series**. Treat young readers to a book talk or read-aloud and watch Henry go flying off the shelf." —*Bulletin of the Center for Children's Books*

"I have tried out the Horrid Henry books with groups of children as a parent, as a baby-sitter, and as a teacher. **Children love to either hear them read aloud or to read them themselves**." —Danielle Hall, teacher

"A flicker of recognition must pass through most teachers and parents when they read Horrid Henry. **There's a tiny bit of him in all of us**." —Nancy Astee, *Child Education*

"**As a teacher...it's great to get a series of books my class loves**. They go mad for Horrid Henry." —teacher

"**Short, easy-to-read chapters will appeal to early readers, who will laugh at Henry's exaggerated antics and relate to his rambunctious personality**." —*School Library Journal*

"An absolutely fantastic series and surely a winner with all children. Long live Francesca Simon and her brilliant books! More, more please!"

—parent

"**Laugh-out-loud reading for both adults and children alike**." —parent

"**Henry's over-the-top behavior, the characters' snappy dialogue and Ross's hyperbolic line art will engage even the most reluctant readers—there's little reason to suspect the series won't conquer these shores as well**." —*Publishers Weekly*

Horrid Henry by Francesca Simon

HORRID HENRY ROCKS

Francesca Simon
Illustrated by Tony Ross

Text © Francesca Simon 2010
Cover and internal illustrations © Tony Ross 2010
Cover and internal design © 2011 by Sourcebooks, Inc.

Published by Sourcebooks Jabberwocky, an imprint of Sourcebooks, Inc.
P.O. Box 4410, Naperville, Illinois 60567-4410
(630) 961-3900
Fax: (630) 961-2168
www.jabberwockykids.com

Originally published in Great Britain in 2010 by Orion Children's Books.

Library of Congress Cataloging-in-Publication data is on file with the publisher.

Source of Production: East Peoria, Illinois, USA
Date of Production: September 2011
Run Number: 16166

Printed and bound in the United States of America.
VP 10 9 8 7 6 5 4 3

For Jesse Nunn,
a major-league Horrid Henry fan,
and for Imogen Stubbs

CONTENTS

1

HORRID HENRY'S INVASION

"Baa! Baa! Baa!"

Perfect Peter baaed happily at his sheep collection. There they were, his ten lovely little sheepies, all beautifully lined up from biggest to smallest, heads facing forward, fluffy tails against the wall, all five centimeters apart from one another, all—

Perfect Peter gasped. Something was wrong. Something was terribly wrong. But what? What? Peter scanned the mantelpiece. Then he saw…

Nooooo!

Fluff Puff, his favorite sheep, the one with the pink and yellow nose, was facing the wrong way around. His nose was shoved against the wall. His tail was facing forward. And he was… he was…crooked!

This could only mean…this could only mean…

"Mom!" screamed Peter. "Mom! Henry was in my room again!"

"Henry!" shouted Mom. "Keep out of Peter's room."

"I'm not in Peter's room," yelled Horrid Henry. "I'm in mine."

"But he was," wailed Peter.

"Was not!" bellowed Horrid Henry.

Tee-hee.

Horrid Henry was strictly forbidden to go into Peter's bedroom without Peter's permission. But sometimes, thought Horrid Henry, when Peter was being even more of a toady toad than usual, he had no choice but to invade.

Peter had run blabbing to Mom that Henry had watched *Mutant Max* and *Knight Fight* when Mom had said he could only watch one or the other. Henry had been banned from watching TV all day. Peter was such a tattletale frogface ninnyhammer toady poo bag, thought Horrid Henry grimly. Well, just wait till Peter tried to color in his new picture, he'd—

"MOM!" screamed Peter. "Henry switched the caps on my markers. I just put pink in the sky."

"Did not!" yelled Henry.

"Did too!" wailed Peter.

"Prove it," said Horrid Henry, smirking.

Mom came upstairs. Quickly Henry leaped over the mess covering the floor of his room, flopped on his bed, and

grabbed a *Screamin' Demon* comic. Peter
came and stood in the doorway.

"Henry's being horrid," sniveled Peter.

"Henry, have you been in Peter's
room?" said Mom.

Henry sighed loudly. "Of course I've
been in his smelly room. I live here,
don't I?"

"I mean when he wasn't there," said Mom.

"No," said Horrid Henry. This wasn't a lie, because even if Peter *wasn't* there his horrible stinky smell was.

"He has too," said Peter. "Fluff Puff was turned the wrong way around."

"Maybe he was just trying to escape from your stinky pants," said Henry. "*I* would."

"Mom!" said Peter.

"Henry! Don't be horrid. Leave your brother alone."

"I *am* leaving him alone," said Horrid Henry. "Why can't he leave *me* alone? And get out of *my* room, Peter!" he shrieked as Peter put his foot just inside Henry's door.

Peter quickly withdrew his foot.

Henry glared at Peter.

Peter glared at Henry.

Mom sighed. "The next one who goes into the other's room without permission will be banned from the computer for a week. And no allowance either."

She turned to go.

Henry stuck out his tongue at Peter.

"Tattletale," he mouthed.

"Mom!" screamed Peter.

Perfect Peter stalked back to his bedroom. How dare Henry sneak in and mess up his sheep? What a mean, horrible brother. Perhaps he needed to calm down and listen to a little music. The *Daffy and her Dancing Daisies Greatest Hits* CD always cheered him up.

"Dance and prance. Prance and dance.
You say moo moo. We say baa.
Everybody says moo moo baa baa,"
piped Perfect Peter as he put on the
Daffy CD.

**Boils on your fat face
Boils make you dumb.
Chop Chop Chop 'em off
Stick 'em on your bum!**

blared the CD player.

Huh? What was that horrible song?
Peter yanked out the CD. It was the
Skullbangers singing the horrible "Bony
Boil" song. Henry must have sneaked a
Skullbanger CD inside the Daffy case.
How dare he? How dare he? Peter
would storm straight downstairs and
tell Mom. Henry would get into big
trouble. Big, big trouble.

Then Peter paused. There *was* the
teeny-tiny possibility that Peter had

mixed them up by mistake…No.
He needed absolute proof of Henry's
horridness. He'd do his homework, then
have a good look around Henry's room
to see if his Daffy CD was hidden there.

Peter glanced at his to-do list pinned
on his bulletin board. When he'd
written it that morning it read:

Peter's To Do List
Practice cello
Fold clothes and put away
Do homework
Brush my teeth
Read Bunny's Big Boo Boo

The list now read:

Peter's To Do List
Practice ~~cello~~ belly dancing
unFold clothes and ~~put~~ away
Throw
Don't ~~do~~ homework
~~Flush~~ my teeth ~~down the toilet~~
Read Bunny's Big Poo Poo

At the bottom someone had added:

Pick my nose
Pinch mom
Give Henry all my money

Well, here was proof! He was going to go straight down and tell on Henry.

"Mom! Henry was in my room again. He scribbled all over my to-do list."

"Henry!" screamed Mom. "I am sick and tired of this! Keep out of your brother's bedroom! This is your last warning! No playing on the computer for a week!"

SNEAK. SNEAK. SNEAK.

Horrid Henry slipped inside the enemy's bedroom. He'd pay Peter back for getting him banned from the computer.

There was Peter's cello. Ha! It only took a moment to unwind all the strings. Now, what else, what else? He could switch around Peter's underpants and sock drawers.

No! Even better. Quickly Henry undid all of Peter's socks and mismatched them. Who said socks should match?

Tee hee. Peter would go crazy when he found out he was wearing one Sammy the Snail sock with one Daffy sock. Then Henry snatched Bunnykins off Peter's bed and crept out.

SNEAK. SNEAK. SNEAK.

Perfect Peter crept down the hall and stood outside Henry's bedroom, holding a muddy twig. His heart was pounding. Peter knew he was strictly forbidden to go into Henry's room without permission. But Henry kept breaking that rule. So why shouldn't he?

Squaring his shoulders, Peter tiptoed in.

CRUNCH.
CRUNCH.
CRUNCH.

Henry's room was a pigsty, thought Perfect Peter, wading through broken knights, crumpled candy wrappers, dirty clothes, ripped comics, and muddy shoes.

Mr. Kill. He'd steal Mr. Kill. Ha! Serve Henry right. And he'd put the muddy twig in Henry's bed. Serve him double right. Perfect Peter grabbed Mr. Kill, shoved the twig in Henry's bed, and dashed back to his room.

And screamed.

Fluff Puff wasn't just turned the wrong way, he was—gone! Henry must have stolen him. And Lambykins was gone

too. And Squish. Peter only had seven
sheep left.

And where was his Bunnykins? He
wasn't on the bed where he belonged.
No!!!!!! This was the last straw. This
was war.

The coast was clear. Peter always took
forever in the bath. Horrid Henry
slipped into the worm's room.

He'd pay Peter back for stealing Mr.
Kill. There he was, shoved in the back
of Peter's closet, where Peter always hid
things he didn't want Henry to find.
Well, ha ha ha, thought Horrid Henry,
rescuing Mr. Kill.

Now what to do, what to do?
Horrid Henry scooped up all of Peter's
remaining sheep and shoved them inside
Peter's pillowcase.

What else? Henry glanced round Peter's immaculate room. He could mess it up. Nah, thought Henry. Peter loved tidying. He could—aha.

Peter had pinned drawings all over the wall above his bed. Henry surveyed them. Shame, thought Henry, that Peter's pictures were all so dull. I mean, really, "My Family," and "My Bunnykins." Horrid Henry climbed on Peter's bed to reach the drawings.

Poor Peter, thought Horrid Henry. What a terrible artist he was. No wonder he was such a smelly toad if he had to look at such awful pictures all the time. Perhaps Henry could improve them...

Now, let's see, thought Horrid Henry, getting out some crayons. Drawing a crown on my head would

be a big improvement. There! That
livens things up. And a big red nose on
Peter would help too, thought Henry,
drawing away. So would a droopy
mustache on Mom. And as for that
stupid picture of Bunnykins, well,
why not draw a lovely toilet for
him to—

"What are you doing in here?" came
a little voice.

Horrid Henry turned.

There was Peter, in his bunny
pajamas, glaring at him.

Uh-oh. If Peter told on him again,
Henry would be in big, big, mega-big
trouble. Mom would probably ban him
from the computer forever.

"You're in my room. I'm telling on
you," shrieked Peter.

"Shhh!" hissed Horrid Henry.

"What do you mean, shhh?" said

Peter. "I'm going straight down to tell Mom."

"One word and you're dead, worm," said Horrid Henry. "Quick! Close the door."

Perfect Peter looked behind him. "Why?"

"Just do it, worm," hissed Henry.

Perfect Peter shut the door.

"What are you doing?" he demanded.

"Dusting for fingerprints," said Horrid Henry smoothly.

Fingerprints?

"What?" said Peter.

"I thought I heard someone in your room, and ran in to check you were okay. Just look what I found," said Horrid Henry dramatically, pointing to Peter's now empty mantelpiece.

Peter let out a squeal.

"My sheepies!" wailed Peter.

"I think there's a burglar in the house,"
whispered Horrid Henry urgently. "And
I think he's hiding…in your room."

Peter gulped. A burglar? In his room?

"A burglar?"

"Yup," said Henry. "Who do you
think stole Bunnykins? And all
your sheep?"

"You," said Peter.

Horrid Henry snorted. "No! What
would I want with your stupid sheep?
But a sheep rustler would love them."

18

Perfect Peter hesitated. Could Henry be telling the truth? *Could* a burglar really have stolen his sheep?

"I think he's hiding under the bed," hissed Horrid Henry. "Why don't you check?"

Peter stepped back.

"No," said Peter. "I'm scared."

"Then get out of here as quick as you can," whispered Henry. "*I'll* check."

"Thank you, Henry," said Peter.

Perfect Peter crept into the hallway. Then he stopped. Something wasn't right…something was a little bit wrong.

Perfect Peter marched back into his bedroom. Henry was by the door.

"I think the burglar is hiding in your closet, I'll get—"

"You said you were fingerprinting," said Peter suspiciously. "With what?"

"My fingers," said Horrid Henry. "Why do you think it's called *finger*printing?"

Then Peter caught sight of his drawings.

"You've ruined my pictures!" shrieked Peter.

"It wasn't me; it must have been the burglar," said Horrid Henry.

"You're trying to trick me," said Peter. "I'm telling!"

Time for Plan B.

"I'm only in here 'cause you were in my room," said Henry.

"Was not!"

"Were too!"

"Liar!"

"Liar!"

"You stole Bunnykins!"

"You stole Mr. Kill!"

"Thief!"

"Thief!"

"I'm telling on you."

"I'm telling on you!"

Henry and Peter glared at each other.

"Okay," said Horrid Henry. "I won't invade your room if you won't invade mine."

"Okay," said Perfect Peter. He'd agree to anything to get Henry to leave his sheep alone.

Horrid Henry smirked.

He couldn't wait until tomorrow when Peter tried to play his cello... tee-hee.

Wouldn't he get a shock!

2

....

MOODY MARGARET'S SLEEPOVER

"What are you doing here?" said Moody Margaret, glaring.

"I'm here for the sleepover," said Sour Susan, glaring back.

"You were uninvited, remember?" said Margaret.

"And then you invited me again, remember?" snapped Susan.

"Did not."

"Did too. You told me last week I could come."

"Did not."

"Did too. You're such a meanie,

Margaret," scowled Susan. Aaaarrggghh. Why was she friends with such a moody old grouch?

Moody Margaret heaved a heavy sigh. Why was she friends with such a sour old slop bucket?

"Well, since you're here, I guess you'd better come in," said Margaret. "But don't expect any dessert 'cause there won't be enough for you and my *real* guests."

Sour Susan stomped inside Margaret's house. Grrrr. She wouldn't be inviting Margaret to her next sleepover party, that's for sure.

Horrid Henry couldn't sleep. He was hot. He was hungry.

"Cookies!" moaned his tummy. "Give me cookies!"

Because Mom and Dad were the

meanest, most
horrible parents in
the world, they'd
forgotten to buy
more cookies
and there wasn't
a single solitary
crumb in the house.
Henry knew because
he'd searched everywhere.

"Give me cookies!" growled his
tummy. "What are you waiting for?"

I'm going to die of hunger up here,
thought Horrid Henry. And it will be
all Mom and Dad's fault. They'll come
in tomorrow morning and find just a
few wisps of hair and some teeth. Then
they'd be sorry. Then they'd wail and
gnash. But it would be too late.

"How could we have forgotten to buy
chocolate cookies?" Dad would sob.

"We deserve to be locked up forever!"
Mom would shriek.

"And now there's nothing left of
Henry but a tooth, and it's all our fault!"
they'd howl.

Humph. Serve them right.

Wait. What an idiot he was. Why
should he risk death from starvation
when he knew where there was a rich
stash of all sorts of yummy cookies
waiting just for him?

Moody Margaret's Secret Club tent
was sure to be full to bursting with

goodies! Horrid Henry hadn't raided it in ages. And so long as he was quick, no one would ever know he'd left the house.

"Go on, Henry," urged his tummy. "FEED ME!"

Horrid Henry didn't need to be urged twice.

Slowly, quietly, he sneaked out of bed, crept down the stairs, and tiptoed out of the back door. Then quick over the wall, and ta-da, he was in the Secret Club tent. There was Margaret's Secret Club cookie tin, in her pathetic hiding place under a blanket. Ha!

Horrid Henry prized open the lid. Oh wow. It was filled to the brim with

Chocolate Fudge Chewies! And those
scrumptious Triple Chocolate Chip
Marshmallow Squidgies! Henry scooped
up a huge handful and stuffed them in
his mouth.

Chomp. Chomp. Chomp.

Oh wow. Oh wow. Was there anything
more delicious in the whole wide world
than a mouthful of stolen cookies?

"More! More! More!" yelped his
tummy.

Who was Horrid Henry to say no?

Henry reached in to snatch another mega handful…

BANG! SLAM! BANG!

STOMP! STOMP! STOMP!

"That's too bad, Gurinder," snapped Margaret's voice. "It's my party so I decide. Hurry up, Susan."

"I am hurrying," said Susan's voice.

The footsteps were heading straight for the Secret Club tent.

Yikes. What was Margaret doing outside at this time of night? There wasn't a moment to lose.

Horrid Henry looked around wildly. Where could he hide? There was a wicker chest at the back, where Margaret kept her dress-up clothes. Horrid Henry leaped inside and pulled the lid shut. Hopefully, the girls wouldn't be long and he could escape

home before Mom and Dad discovered
he'd been out.

Moody Margaret bustled into the
tent, followed by her mother, Gorgeous
Gurinder, Kung-Fu Kate, Lazy Linda,
Vain Violet, Singing Soraya, and
Sour Susan.

"Now, girls, it's late, I want you to go
straight to bed, lights out, no talking,"
said Margaret's mother. "My little Maggie
Moo Moo needs her beauty sleep."

Ha, thought Horrid Henry. Margaret could sleep for a thousand years and she'd still look like a frog.

"Yes, Mom," said Margaret.

"Good night, girls," trilled Margaret's mom. "See you in the morning."

Phew, thought Horrid Henry, lying as still as he could. He'd be back home in no time, mission safely accomplished.

"We're sleeping out here?" said Singing Soraya. "In a tent?"

"I said it was a Secret Club sleepover," said Margaret.

Horrid Henry's heart sank. Huh? They were planning to sleep here? Rats, rats, rats, double rats. He was going to have to hide inside this hot dusty chest until they were asleep.

Maybe they'd all fall asleep soon, thought Horrid Henry hopefully.

Because he had to get home before Mom and Dad discovered he was missing. If they realized he'd sneaked outside, he'd be in so much trouble his life wouldn't be worth living and he might as well abandon all hope of ever watching TV or eating another cookie until he was an old, shriveled bag of bones struggling to chew with his one tooth and watch TV with his magnifying glass and hearing aid. Yikes!

Horrid Henry looked grimly at the cookies clutched in his fist. Thank goodness he'd brought provisions.

He might be trapped here for a very
long time.

"Where's your sleeping bag, Violet?"
said Margaret.

"I didn't bring one," said Vain Violet.
"I don't like sleeping on the floor."

"Tough," said Margaret, "that's where
we're sleeping."

"But I need to sleep in a bed," whined
Vain Violet. "I don't want to sleep
out here."

"Well, we do," said Margaret.

"Yeah," said Susan.

"I can sleep anywhere," said Lazy Linda, yawning.

"I'm calling my mom," said Violet. "I want to go home."

"Go ahead," said Margaret. "We don't need you, do we?"

Silence.

"Oh come on, Violet, stay," said Gurinder.

"Yeah, stay," said Kung-Fu Kate.

"No!" said Violet, flouncing out of the tent.

"Hummph," said Moody Margaret.

36

"She's no fun anyway. Now, everyone put your sleeping bags down where I say. I need to sleep by the entrance, because I need fresh air."

"I want to sleep by the entrance," said Soraya.

"No," said Margaret, "it's my party so I decide. Susan, you go to the back because you snore."

"Do not," said Susan.

"Do too," said Margaret.

"Liar."

"Liar."

SLAP!

SLAP!

"That's it!" wailed Susan. "I'm calling my mom."

"Go ahead," said Margaret, "see if I care, snore-box. That'll be tons more Chocolate Fudge Chewies for the rest of us."

Sour Susan stood still. She'd been looking forward to Margaret's sleep-over for ages. And she still hadn't had any of the midnight feast Margaret had promised.

"All right, I'll stay," said Susan sourly, putting her sleeping bag down at the back of the tent by the dress-up chest.

"I want to be next to Gurinder," said Lazy Linda, scratching her head.

"Do you have lice?" said Gurinder.

"No!" said Linda.

"You do too," said Gurinder.

"Do not," said Linda.

"Do too," said Gurinder. "I'm not sleeping next to someone who has lice."

"Me neither," said Kate.

"Me neither," said Soraya.

"Don't look at me," said Margaret. "I'm not sleeping next to you."

"I don't have lice!" wailed Linda.

"Go next to Susan," said Margaret.

"But she snores," protested Linda.

"But she has lice," protested Susan.

"Do not."

"Do not."

"Bedbug head."

"Snory!"

Suddenly something scuttled across the floor.

"EEEEK!" squealed Soraya. "It's a mouse!" She scrambled onto the dress-up chest. The lid sagged.

"It won't hurt you," said Margaret.

"Yeah," said Susan.

"Eeeek!" squealed Linda, shrinking back. The lid sagged even more.

Cree—eaaak went the chest.

Aaarrrrggghhh, thought Horrid Henry, trying to squash himself down before he was squished.

"Eeeek!" squealed Gurinder, scrambling onto the chest.

CREE—EAAAAAK! went the chest.

Errrrgh, thought Horrid Henry, pushing up against the sagging lid as hard as he could.

"I can't sleep if there's a…mouse," said Gurinder. She looked around nervously. "What if it runs on top of my sleeping bag?"

Margaret sighed. "It's only a mouse," she said.

"I'm scared of mice," whimpered Gurinder. "I'm leaving!" And she ran out of the tent, wailing.

"More food for the rest of us," said Margaret, shrugging. "I say we feast now."

"About time," said Soraya.

"Let's start with the Chocolate Fudge Chewies," said Margaret, opening the Secret Club cookie tin. "Everyone can

41

have two, except for me, I get four
'cause it's my..."

Margaret peered into the tin. There
were only a few crumbs inside.

"Who stole the cookies?" said
Margaret.

"Wasn't me," said Susan.

"Wasn't me," said Soraya.

"Wasn't me," said Kate.

"Wasn't me," said Linda.

Tee-hee, thought Horrid Henry.

"One of you did, so no one is getting anything to eat until you admit it," snapped Margaret.

"Meanie," muttered Susan sourly.

"What did you say?" said Moody Margaret.

"Nothing," said Susan.

"Then we'll just have to wait for the culprit to come forward," said Margaret, scowling. "Meanwhile, get in your sleeping bags. We're going to tell scary stories in the dark. Who knows a good one?"

"I do," said Susan.

"Not the story about the ghost kitty cat that drank up all the milk in your kitchen, is it?" said Margaret.

Susan scowled.

"Well, it's a true scary story," said Susan.

"I know a real scary story," said Kung-Fu Kate. "It's about this monster—"

"Mine's better," said Margaret. "It's about a flesh-eating zombie that creeps around at night and rips off—"

"NOOOO," wailed Linda. "I hate being scared. I'm calling my mom to come and get me."

"No scaredy-cats allowed in the Secret Club," said Margaret.

"I don't care," said Linda, flouncing out.

"It's not a sleepover unless we tell ghost stories," said Moody Margaret. "Turn off your flashlights. It won't be scary unless we're all sitting in the dark."

Sniffle. Sniffle. Sniffle.

"I want to go home," sniveled Soraya.

"I've never slept away from home before…I want my mommy."

"What a baby," said Moody Margaret.

Horrid Henry was cramped and hot and uncomfortable. Pins and needles were shooting up his arm. He shifted his shoulder, brushing against the lid.

There was a muffled creak.

Henry froze. Whoops. Henry prayed they hadn't heard anything.

"…and the zombie crept inside the tent, gnashing its bloody teeth and sniffing the air for human flesh, hungry for more—"

Ow. His poor aching arm. Henry shifted position again.

Creak…

"What was that?" whispered Susan.

"What was what?" said Margaret.

"There was a…a…creak…" said Susan.

"The wind," said Margaret. "Anyway, the zombie sneaked into the tent and—"

"You don't think…" hissed Kate.

"Think what?" said Margaret.

"That the zombie…the zombie…"

I'm starving, thought Horrid Henry.

I'll just eat a few cookies really, really, really quietly—

Crunch. Crunch.

"What was that?" whispered Susan.

"What was what?" said Margaret. "You're ruining the story."

"That…crunching sound," hissed Susan.

Horrid Henry gasped. What an idiot he was! Why hadn't he thought of this before?

Crunch. Crunch. Crunch.

"Like someone…someone…crunching on…bones," whispered Kung-Fu Kate.

"Someone…here…" whispered Susan.

Tap. Horrid Henry rapped on the underside of the lid.

Tap! Tap! Tap!

"I didn't hear anything," said Margaret loudly.

"It's the zombie!" screamed Susan.

"He's in here!" screamed Kate. AAAAARRRRRRRGHHHHHHH!"

"I'm going home!" screamed Susan and Kate. "MOMMMMMMMMYYYY!" they wailed, running off.

Ha ha, thought Horrid Henry. His brilliant plan had worked!!! Tee-hee. He'd hop out, steal the rest of the feast and scoot home. Hopefully Mom and Dad—

YANK!

Suddenly the chest lid was flung open and a flashlight shone in his eyes.

Moody Margaret's hideous face glared down at him.

"Gotcha!" said Moody Margaret. "Oh boy, are you in trouble. Just wait till I tell on you. Ha ha, Henry, you're dead."

Horrid Henry climbed out of the chest and brushed a few crumbs onto the rug.

"Just wait till I tell everyone at school about your sleepover," said Horrid Henry. "How you were so mean and bossy everyone ran away."

"Your parents will punish you forever," said Moody Margaret.

"Your name will be mud forever," said Horrid Henry. "Everyone will laugh at you and serves you right, Maggie Moo Moo."

"Don't call me that," said Margaret, glaring.

49

"Call you what, Moo Moo?"

"All right," said Margaret slowly. "I won't tell on you if you give me two packs of Chocolate Fudge Chewies."

"No way," said Henry. "I won't tell on you if you give me three packs of Chocolate Fudge Chewies."

"Fine," said Margaret. "Your parents are still up, I'll tell them where you are right now. I wouldn't want them to worry."

"Go ahead," said Henry. "I can't wait until school tomorrow."

Margaret scowled.

"Just this once," said Horrid Henry. "I won't tell on you if you won't tell on me."

"Just this once," said Moody Margaret. "But never again."

They glared at each other.

When he was king, thought Horrid

Henry, anyone named Margaret would
be catapulted over the walls into an
oozy swamp. Meanwhile…on guard,
Margaret. On guard. I will be avenged!

3

···

HORRID HENRY'S AUTOBIOGRAPHY

Bang! Crash! Kaboom!

Rude Ralph bounced on a chair and did his Tarzan impression.

Moody Margaret yanked Lazy Linda's hair. Linda screamed.

Stone-Age Steven stomped around the room grunting "Ugg."

"Rat about town
don't need a gown.
Where I'm goin'
Only fangs'll be showin,"

shrieked Horrid Henry.

"Quiet!" barked Miss Battle-Axe. "Settle down immediately."

Ralph bounced.

Steven stomped.

Linda screamed.

Henry shrieked. He was the Killer
Boy Rats new lead singer, blasting
his music into the roaring crowd,
hurling—

"HENRY, BE QUIET!" bellowed
Miss Battle-Axe. "Or playtime is
canceled. For everyone."

Horrid Henry scowled. Why oh
why did he have to come to school?
Why didn't the Killer Boy Rats start
a school, where you'd do nothing but
scream and stomp all day? Now that's
the sort of school everyone would
want to go to. But no. He had to
come here. When he was king all
schools would just teach jousting
and spying and Terminator Gladiator
would be principal.

Henry looked at the clock. How could it be only 9:42? It felt like he'd been sitting here for ages. What he'd give to be lounging right now on the comfy black chair, eating chips and watching *Hog House*...

"Today we have a very exciting project," said Miss Battle-Axe.

Henry groaned. Miss Battle-Axe's idea of an exciting project and his were never the same. An exciting project

would be building a time machine, or a
"let's see who can give Henry the most
chocolate" competition, or counting
how many times he could hit Miss
Battle-Axe with a water balloon.

"We'll be writing autobiographies,"
said Miss Battle-Axe.

Ha. He knew it would be something
boring. Horrid Henry hated writing.
All that pushing a pen across a piece
of paper. Writing always made his
hand ache. Writing was hard, heavy

work. Why did Miss Battle-Axe try to torture him every day? Didn't she have anything better to do? Henry groaned again.

"An autobiography means the story of your life," continued Miss Battle-Axe, glaring at him with her evil red eyes. "Everyone will write a page about themselves and all the interesting things they've done."

Yawn. Could his life get any worse?

Write a page? A whole entire page? What could be more boring then writing on and on about himself—

Wait a minute.

He got to write…about himself? The world's most fascinating boy? He could write for hours about himself! Days. Weeks. Years. Hold on…what was batty old Miss Battle-Axe saying now?

"…the really exciting part is that our

autobiographies will be published in the local newspaper next week."

Oh wow! Oh wow! Oh wow! His autobiography would be published!

This was his chance to tell the world all about being Lord High Excellent Majesty of the Purple Hand Gang. How he'd vanquished so many evil enemies. All the brilliant tricks he'd played on Peter. He'd write about the Mega-Mean Time Machine. And the Fangmangler. And the millions of times he'd defeated the Secret Club and squished Moody Margaret to a pulp! And oh yes, he'd be sure to include the time he'd turned his one line in the school play into a starring part and scored the winning goal in the class soccer game. But one page would barely cover one day in his life. He needed hundreds of pages...no, thousands of pages to write about just some of his top triumphs.

Where to begin?

"Let's start with you, Clare," burbled Miss Battle-Axe. "What would you put in your autobiography?"

Clare beamed. "I walked when I was four months old, learned to read when I was two, did long division when I was three, built my first telescope when I was four, composed a symphony—"

"Thank you, Clare, I'm sure everyone will look forward to learning more about you," said Miss Battle-Axe. "Steven. What will—"

"Can't we just get started?" shouted Henry. "I've got masses to write."

"As I was saying, before I was so RUDELY interrupted," said Miss Battle-Axe, glaring, "Steven, what will you be writing about in your autobiography?"

"Being a caveman," grunted Stone-Age Steven. "Uggg."

"Fascinating," said Miss Battle-Axe. "Bert! What's interesting about your life?"

"I dunno," said Beefy Bert.

"Right, then, everyone get to work," said Miss Battle-Axe, fixing Horrid Henry with her basilisk stare.

Horrid Henry wrote until his hand ached. But he'd barely got to the time he tricked Margaret into eating glop before Miss Battle-Axe ordered everyone to stop.

"But I haven't finished!" shouted Horrid Henry.

"Tough," said Miss Battle-Axe. "Now, before we send these autobiographies to the newspaper, I'd like a few of you to read yours aloud to the class. William, let's start with you."

Weepy William burst into tears. "I don't want to go

first," he wailed, dabbing his eyes with some toilet paper.

"Read," said Miss Battle-Axe.

WILLIAM'S AUTOBIOGRAPHY

I was born. I cried. A few years later
my brother, Neil, was born. I cried.
In school Toby broke my pencil.
Margaret picked me last. When we had
to build the Parthenon Henry took all
my paper and then when I got some more
it was dirty. I had to play a blade of grass
in the Nativity play. I cried. I lost every
race on Sports Day. I cried. Then
I got lice. On the school trip to the Ice
Cream Factory I peed in my pants.
I cried. Nothing else has ever
happened to me.

"Who's next?" asked Miss Battle-Axe.
Horrid Henry's hand shot up. Miss

Battle-Axe looked as if a zombie had just walked across her grave. Horrid Henry never put his hand up.

"Linda," said Miss Battle-Axe.

Lazy Linda woke up and yawned.

LINDA'S AUTOBIOGRAPHY

I've had many nice beds in my life. First was my Moses basket. Then my cot. Then my little bed. Then my great big sleigh bed. Then my princess bed with the curtains and the yellow headboard. I've

also had a lot of quilts. First my
quilt had ducks on it. Then I got a
new soft one with big fluffy clouds.
Oooh, I am sleepy just thinking
about it...

"We have time to hear one more,"
said Miss Battle-Axe, scanning the class.
Horrid Henry thought his arm would
detach itself from his shoulder if he
shoved it any higher. "Margaret," said
Miss Battle-Axe.

Henry scowled. It was so unfair. No
one wanted to know about that moody
old grouch.

Moody Margaret swaggered to the
front and noisily cleared her throat.

MARGARET'S AUTOBIOGRAPHY
Greetings, world. I'm very sad when
I think that many of you reading this
will never get to meet someone as

amazing as me. But at least you can read something I've written, and you newspaper people should save this piece of paper, because I, Margaret, have touched it with my very own hands, and it's sure to be valuable in the future when I'm famous.

Let me tell you a few things about marvelous me. First, I am the leader of the Secret Club, which is always victorious against the pathetic and puny Purple Hand Gang next door. One reason we always destroy them, apart from my brilliant plotting, is because the Purple Hand's so-called leader, Henry, is really stupid and useless and pathetic.

Horrid Henry could not believe his ears. "Liar!" shouted Henry. "I always win!" "Shh!" said Miss Battle-Axe.

Naturally, I am the best soccer
player the school has ever had
or will ever have, and naturally
I'm captain of the soccer team.
Everyone always wants to play
on my team, but of course I
don't let no-hopers like Henry
on it. I'm also a fantastic
trumpet player and a top spy.
My best toy is my Dungeon
Drink Kit, which I've used many
times to play great tricks on the
Purple Hand Gang, which they
always fall for.

But I know I'll be very famous
so I'm saving my best stories
for my future bestselling
autobiography. I expect
there will be many
statues built in my

honor all over town, and that this school
will be renamed the Margaret School.

I know it's hard realizing that you can never
be as great as me, but get used to it!!!

Moody Margaret stopped reading and
swaggered to her seat.

"Yay!" yelled Sour Susan.

"Boo!" yelled Horrid Henry.

"Boo!" yelled Rude Ralph.

"There's no booing in this class," said
Miss Battle-Axe.

Horrid Henry was outraged.
Margaret's lies about him…published?
The Purple Hand Gang always won.
But the whole world would believe her
lies once they read them in a newspaper.
He had to stop that foul fiend. He had
to show everyone what a big fat liar
Margaret really was.

But how? How? He could just try to steal her autobiography. But someone might notice it had gone missing. Or he could…he could…

The playtime bell rang. Miss Battle-Axe starting collecting up all the autobiographies. Henry watched helplessly as Margaret's pack of boasting lies went into the folder.

And then Horrid Henry knew what he had to do. It was dangerous. It was risky. But a pirate gang leader had to take his chances, come what may.

Horrid Henry put up his hand. "Please, miss, I haven't finished my autobiography yet. Could I stay in at playtime to finish?"

Miss Battle-Axe looked at Henry as if he had just grown an extra head. Henry...asking to spend more time on work? Horrid Henry asking to skip playtime?

"You can have five more minutes," said Miss Battle-Axe, mopping her brow.

Horrid Henry wrote and wrote and wrote. When would Miss Battle-Axe leave him alone for a moment? But there she was, stapling up drawings of light bulbs.

"Put it in the folder with the others," said Miss Battle-Axe, facing the wall. Horrid Henry didn't wait to be asked twice and grabbed the folder.

There wasn't a moment to lose. Henry rifled through the autobiographies, removed Margaret's, and substituted his new, improved version.

Moody Margaret peered round the door. Tee-hee, thought Horrid Henry, pushing past her. Wouldn't she get a

shock when she got her newspaper!
What he'd give to see her face.

THWACK!

The local paper dropped through the
door. Henry snatched it. There was
the headline:

LOCAL CHILDREN SHINE
IN FASCINATING TALES OF
THEIR LIVES

Feverishly, he turned to read the class
autobiographies.

MARGARET'S AUTOBIOGRAPHY

**Oh woe is me, to be such a silly
moody grouchy grump. I've always
looked like a frog, in fact my mom
took one look at me when I was
born, threw me in the garbage and
ran screaming from the room. I don't
blame her; I scream too whenever I
see my ugly warty face in the mirror.**

Everyone calls me Maggie Moo Moo, or Maggie Poo Poo, because I still wear diapers. I started a Secret Club, which no one wants to join, because I am so mean and bossy.

I can't even have a sleepover without everyone running away. I keep trying to beat Henry's Purple Hand Gang, but he's much too clever for me and always foils my evil plans. I live next door to Henry, but of course I don't deserve such a great honor. I

**really should just live in a smelly hole
somewhere with all the other frogs.
So, just remember, everyone, beware
of being a moody, grouchy grump, or
you might end up as horrible as me.**

Yes! What a triumph! He was brilliant.
He was a genius. What an amazing trick
to write the truth about Margaret and
swap it for her pack of lies.

Horrid Henry beamed. Now to enjoy
his own autobiography. It was far too
short, but there was always next time.

HENRY'S AUTOBIOGRAPHY
**I'm a total copycat. Luckily, I live
next door to the amazing Margaret,
who I look up to and admire and
worship more than anyone in the
world. Margaret is my heroine, but I
will never be as clever or as brilliant
as she is, because I'm a pathetic,**

useless toad. I copied her amazing
Secret Club, but the Purple Hand
always loses. I tried to do makeovers,
but of course I couldn't. Even my
own brother wants to work for her
as a spy. But then, she is an empress
and I'm a worm.

The most
exciting thing
that ever
happened to
me was when
Margaret
moved in
next door. I hope that one day she
will let me be the guard of the Secret
Club, but I will have to work very
hard to deserve it. That would be the
best thing that has ever happened in
my boring life.

Huh? What? That fiend! That foul fiend!

The doorbell rang.

There was Margaret, waving the newspaper. Her face was purple.

"How dare you!" she shrieked.

"How dare you!" Henry shrieked.

"I'll get you for this, Henry," hissed Margaret.

"Just you wait, Margaret," hissed Henry.

4

HORRID HENRY ROCKS

"Boys, I have a very special treat for you," said Mom, beaming.

Horrid Henry looked up from his *Mutant Max* comic.

Perfect Peter looked up from his spelling homework.

A treat? A special treat? A very special treat? Maybe Mom and Dad were finally appreciating him. Maybe they'd got tickets…maybe they'd actually got tickets…Horrid Henry's heart leaped. Could it be possible that at last, at long last, he'd get to go to a Killer Boy Rats concert?

"We're going to the Daffy and her Dancing Daisies show!" said Mom. "I got the last four tickets."

"OOOOOOHHHH," said Peter, clapping his hands. "Yippee! I love Daffy."

What?? NOOOOOOOOOOOO! That wasn't a treat. That was torture. A treat would be a day at the Frosty Freeze Ice Cream Factory. A treat would be no school. A treat would be all he could eat at Gobble and Go.

"I don't want to see that stupid Daffy," said Horrid Henry. "I want to see the Killer Boy Rats."

"No way," said Mom.

"I don't like the Killer Boy Rats," shuddered Peter. "Too scary."

"Me neither," shuddered Mom. "Too loud."

"Me neither," shuddered Dad. "Too shouty."

"NOOOOOOOO!" screamed Henry.

"But Henry," said Peter, "everyone loves Daffy."

"Not me," snarled Henry.

Perfect Peter waved a flier. "Daffy's going to be the greatest show ever. Read this."

Daffy sings and dances her way across the stage and into your heart. Your chance to sing-along to all your favorite daisy songs! I'm a Lazy Daisy. Whoops-a-Daisy. And of course, Upsy-Daisy, Crazy Daisy, Prance and Dance-a-Daisy.

✱

With special guest star Busy Lizzie!!!

AAAARRRRRGGGGGGHHHHHH.

Moody Margaret's parents were taking her to the Killer Boy Rats concert. Rude Ralph was going to the Killer Boy Rats concert. Even Anxious Andrew was going, and he didn't even like them. Stuck-Up Steve had been bragging for months that he was going and would be sitting in a special box. It was so unfair.

No one was a bigger Rats fan than Horrid Henry. Henry had all their albums: *Killer Boy Rats Attack-Tack-Tack*, *Killer Boy Rats Splat!*, *Killer Boy Rats Manic Panic*.

"It's not fair!" screamed Horrid Henry. "I want to see the Killers!!!!"

"We have to see something that everyone in the family will like," said Mom. "Peter's too young for the Killer Boy Rats but we can all enjoy Daffy."

"Not me!" screamed Henry.

Oh, why did he have such a stupid diaper baby for a brother? Younger brothers should be banned. They just wrecked everything. When he was King Henry the Horrible, all younger brothers would be arrested and dumped in a volcano.

In fact, why wait?

Horrid Henry pounced. He was a fiery god scooping up a human sacrifice and hurling him into the volcano's molten depths.

"AAAIIIIIEEEEEEE!" screamed
Perfect Peter. "Henry attacked me."

"Stop being horrid, Henry!" shouted
Mom. "Leave your brother alone."

"I won't go to Daffy," yelled Henry.
"And you can't make me."

"Go to your room," said Dad.

Horrid Henry paced up and down his
bedroom, singing his favorite Rats song
at the top of his lungs:

"I'm dead, you're dead, we're dead.
Get over it.
Dead is great, dead's where it's at
'Cause..."

"Henry! Be quiet!" screamed Dad.

"I am being quiet!" bellowed Henry. Honestly. Now, how could he get out of going to that terrible Daffy concert? He'd easily be the oldest one there. Only stupid babies liked Daffy. If the horrible songs didn't kill him then he was sure to die of embarrassment. Then they'd be sorry they'd made him go. But it would be too late. Mom and Dad and Peter could sob and boohoo all they liked but he'd still be dead. And serve them right for being so mean to him.

Dad said if he was good he could see the Killer Boys next time they were in town. Ha. The Killer Boy Rats NEVER put on concerts. Next time they did

he'd be old and hobbling and whacking
Peter with his cane.

He had to get a Killer Boys ticket
now. He just had to. But how? They'd
been sold out for weeks.

Maybe he could place an ad:

Can you help?

Deserving boy suffering from rare and terrible
illness. His ears are falling off. Doctor has prescribed
the Killer Boy Rats cure. Only by hearing the Rats
live is there any hope. If you've got a ticket to the
concert on Saturday PLEASE send it to Henry NOW.
(If you don't you know you'll be sorry.)

That might work. Or he could tell people that the concert was cursed and anyone who went would turn into a rat. Hmmm. Somehow Henry didn't see Margaret falling for that. Too bad Peter didn't have a ticket, thought Henry sadly, he could tell him he'd turn into a killer and Peter would hand over the ticket instantly.

And then suddenly Horrid Henry had a brilliant, spectacular idea. There must be someone out there who was desperate for a Daffy ticket. In fact there must be someone out there who would swap a Killers ticket for a Daffy one. It was certainly worth a try.

"Hey, Brian, I hear you've got a Killer Boy Rats ticket," said Horrid Henry at school the next day.

"So?" said Brainy Brian.

"I've got a ticket to something much better," said Henry.

"What?" said Brian. "The Killers are the best."

Horrid Henry could barely force the grisly words out of his mouth. He twisted his lips into a smile.

"Daffy and her Dancing Daisies," said Horrid Henry.

Brainy Brian stared at him.

"Daffy and her Dancing Daisies?" he spluttered.

"Yes," said Horrid Henry brightly. "I've heard it's their best show ever. Great new songs. You'd love it. Wanna swap?"

Brainy Brian stared at him as if he had a turnip instead of a head.

"You're trying to swap Daffy and her Dancing Daisies tickets for the Killer Boy Rats?" said Brian slowly.

"I'm doing you a favor, no one likes the Killer Boy Rats anymore," said Henry.

"I do," said Brian.

Rats.

"How come you have a ticket for Daffy?" said Brian. "Isn't that a baby show?"

"It's not mine, I found it," said Horrid Henry quickly. Oops.

"Ha ha, Henry, I'm seeing the Killers, and you're not," Margaret taunted.

"Yeah, Henry," said Sour Susan.

"I heard…" Margaret doubled over laughing, "I heard you were going to the Daffy show!"

"That's a big fat lie," said Henry hotly. "I wouldn't be seen dead there."

Horrid Henry looked around the auditorium at the sea of little baby nappy

faces. There was Needy Neil clutching
his mother's hand. There was Weepy
William, crying because he'd dropped
his ice cream. There was Toddler Tom,
up past his bedtime. Oh, no! There was
Lisping Lily. Henry ducked.

Phew. She hadn't seen him. Margaret
would never stop teasing him if she
ever found out. When he was king,
Daffy and her Dancing Daisies would
live in a dungeon with only rats for
company. Anyone who so much as
mentioned the name Daffy, or even
grew a daisy, would be flushed down
the toilet.

There was a round of polite applause
as Daffy and her Dancing Daisies
pirouetted on stage. Horrid Henry
slumped in his seat as far as he could
slump and pulled his cap over his face.
Thank goodness he'd come disguised

and brought some earplugs. No one would ever know he'd been there.

"Tra la la la la la la!" trilled the Daisies.

"Tra la la la la la la!" trilled the audience.

Oh, the torture, groaned Horrid Henry as horrible song followed horrible song. Perfect Peter sang along. So did Mom and Dad.

AAARRRRRGGGHHHHH. And

to think that tomorrow night the Killer
Boy Rats would be performing…and he
wouldn't be there! It was so unfair.

Then Daffy cartwheeled to the front
of the stage. One of the daisies stood
beside her holding a giant hat.

"And now the moment all you Daffy
Daisy fans have been waiting for,"
squealed Daffy. "It's the Lucky Ducky
Daisy Draw, when we call up on stage
an oh-so-lucky audience member to
lead us in the Whoops-a-Daisy sing-
along song! Who's it going to be?"

"Me!" squealed Peter. Mom squeezed
his arm.

Daffy fumbled in the hat and pulled
out a ticket.

"And the lucky winner of our ticket
raffle is…Henry! Ticket 597! Ticket
597, yes, Henry, you in row P, seat 10,
come on up! Daffy needs you on stage!"

Horrid Henry was stuck to his seat in
horror. It must be some other Henry.
Never in his worst nightmares had he
ever imagined—

"Henry, that's you," said Perfect Peter.
"You're so lucky."

"Henry! Come on up, Henry!"
shrieked Daffy. "Don't be shy!"

Onstage at the Daffy show? No! No!

Wait till Moody Margaret found out.
Wait till anyone found out. Henry would
never hear the end of it. He wasn't
moving. Pigs would fly before he budged.

"Henwy!" squealed Lisping Lily
behind him. "Henwy! I want to give
you a big kiss, Henwy…"

Horrid Henry leaped out of his seat.
Lily! Lisping Lily! That fiend in toddler's
clothing would stop at nothing to get
hold of him.

Before Henry knew what had
happened, ushers dressed as daisies had
nabbed him and pushed him onstage.

Horrid Henry blinked in the lights.
Was anyone in the world as unlucky
as he?

"All together now, everyone get ready
to ruffle their petals. Let's sing Tippy-
toe daisy do/Let us sing a song for you!"
beamed Daffy. "Henry, you start us off."

Horrid Henry stared at the vast
audience. Everyone was looking at
him. Of course he didn't know any
stupid Daisy songs. He always blocked
his ears or ran from the room whenever
Peter sang them. Whatever could the
words be…"Watch out, whoop-de-do/
Daisy's doing a big poo?"

These poor stupid kids. If only
they could hear some decent songs,
like…like…

**"Granny on her crutches
Push her off her chair
Shove Shove Shove Shove
Shove her down the stairs."**

shrieked Horrid Henry.

The audience was silent. Daffy looked stunned.

"Uh, Henry…that's not Tippy-toe daisy do," whispered Daffy.

"C'mon everyone, join in with me," shouted Horrid Henry, spinning around and twirling in his best Killer Boy Rats manner.

**"I'm in my coffin
No time for coughin'
When you're squished down dead.
Don't care if you're a goony
Don't care if you're a loony,
Don't care if you're cartoony
I'll squish you!"**

sang Horrid Henry as loud as he could.

**"Gonna be a rock star (and you ain't)
Don't even—"**

Two security guards ran onstage and grabbed Horrid Henry.

"Killer Boy Rats forever!" shrieked Henry as he was dragged off.

★ ★ ★

Horrid Henry stared at the special delivery letter covered in skulls and crossbones. His hand shook.

Hey Henry,
We saw a video of you singing our songs and getting yanked off stage— way to go killer boy! Here's a pair of tickets for our concert tonight, and a backstage pass—see you there.
The Killer Boy Rats

Horrid Henry goggled at the tickets
and the backstage pass. He couldn't
move. He couldn't breathe. He was
going to the Killer Boy Rats concert.
He was actually going to the Killer Boy
Rats concert.

Life, thought Horrid Henry, beaming,
was sweet.

Acknowledgments

Thanks to Hannah Goodwin,
who suggested Horrid Henry's
Autobiography would be a good title
for a story. And thanks to Michael
Rosen for the muddy twig revenge,
and to my son, Josh, who came up
with an extraordinary number
of excellent tricks for Henry
to play on Peter.

About the Author

Photo: Francesco Guidicini

Francesca Simon
spent her childhood
on the beach in
California and then
went to Yale and
Oxford Universities
to study medieval
history and literature. She now lives
in London with her family. She has
written over forty-five books and won
the Children's Book of the Year in 2008
at the Galaxy British Book Awards for
Horrid Henry and the Abominable Snowman.